Dear Parents:

Congratulations! Your child is taking the first steps on an exciting journey. The destination? Independent reading!

STEP INTO READING® will help your child get there. The program offers five steps to reading success. Each step includes fun stories and colorful art or photographs. In addition to original fiction and books with favorite characters, there are Step into Reading Non-Fiction Readers, Phonics Readers and Boxed Sets, Sticker Readers, and Comic Readers—a complete literacy program with something to interest every child.

Learning to Read, Step by Step!

Ready to Read   Preschool–Kindergarten
• big type and easy words • rhyme and rhythm • picture clues
For children who know the alphabet and are eager to begin reading.

Reading with Help   Preschool–Grade 1
• basic vocabulary • short sentences • simple stories
For children who recognize familiar words and sound out new words with help.

Reading on Your Own   Grades 1–3
• engaging characters • easy-to-follow plots • popular topics
For children who are ready to read on their own.

Reading Paragraphs   Grades 2–3
• challenging vocabulary • short paragraphs • exciting stories
For newly independent readers who read simple sentences with confidence.

Ready for Chapters   Grades 2–4
• chapters • longer paragraphs • full-color art
For children who want to take the plunge into chapter books but still like colorful pictures.

STEP INTO READING® is designed to give every child a successful reading experience. The grade levels are only guides; children will progress through the steps at their own speed, developing confidence in their reading. The F&P Text Level on the back cover serves as another tool to help you choose the right book for your child.

Remember, a lifetime love of reading starts with a single step!

For Mrs. Mueller
—C.B.C.

TM & copyright © by Dr. Seuss Enterprises, L.P. 2018

All rights reserved. Published in the United States by Random House Children's Books, a division of Penguin Random House LLC, New York. Featuring characters from *Green Eggs and Ham* by Dr. Seuss, TM & copyright © by Dr. Seuss Enterprises, L.P., 1960, renewed 1988.

Step into Reading, Random House, and the Random House colophon are registered trademarks of Penguin Random House LLC.

Visit us on the Web!
Seussville.com
StepIntoReading.com
rhcbooks.com

Educators and librarians, for a variety of teaching tools, visit us at RHTeachersLibrarians.com

Library of Congress Cataloging-in-Publication Data
Names: Carbone, Courtney, author. | Brannon, Tom, illustrator.
Title: Cooking with Sam-I-Am / by Courtney Carbone ; illustrated by Tom Brannon.
Description: First edition. | New York : Random House, 2018. | Series: Step into reading. Step 1
Summary: Sam-I-Am cooks green eggs and ham with Mouse and Fox.
Identifiers: LCCN 2017018246 | ISBN 978-1-5247-7088-4 (trade) | ISBN 978-1-5247-7089-1 (lib. bdg.)
Subjects: LCSH: Cooking (Eggs)—Fiction. | CYAC: Stories in rhyme.

Printed in the United States of America

10 9 8 7 6 5 4 3 2 1

This book has been officially leveled by using the F&P Text Level Gradient™ Leveling System.

COOKING with SAM-I-AM

by Courtney Carbone

illustrated by Tom Brannon

Random House 🏠 New York

I am Sam.

Sam-I-am.

I want to cook
green eggs and ham.

We can cook them
here or there.

We can cook them
anywhere!

11

Let us cook them
at my house.

Please help
cook them,
Fox and Mouse.

All my eggs
are in this box.

Will you crack
them, Mr. Fox?

Start with butter.

Just a pat.

Put the butter
in a pan.

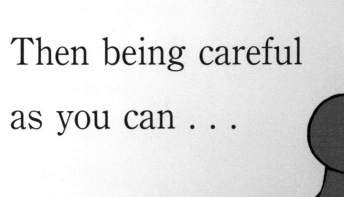

Then being careful

as you can . . .

Crack the eggs.

Watch them cook.

The eggs are ready.

Look! Look! Look!

Now we need
to heat the ham.

Watch and learn
from Sam-I-am!

Turn off the heat.

Take out the meat.

Cut off a piece.

Pull up a seat.

You will like this.

Taste and see.

You will like this
just like me!

It is time

to eat, eat, eat!

Green eggs and ham
cannot be beat!